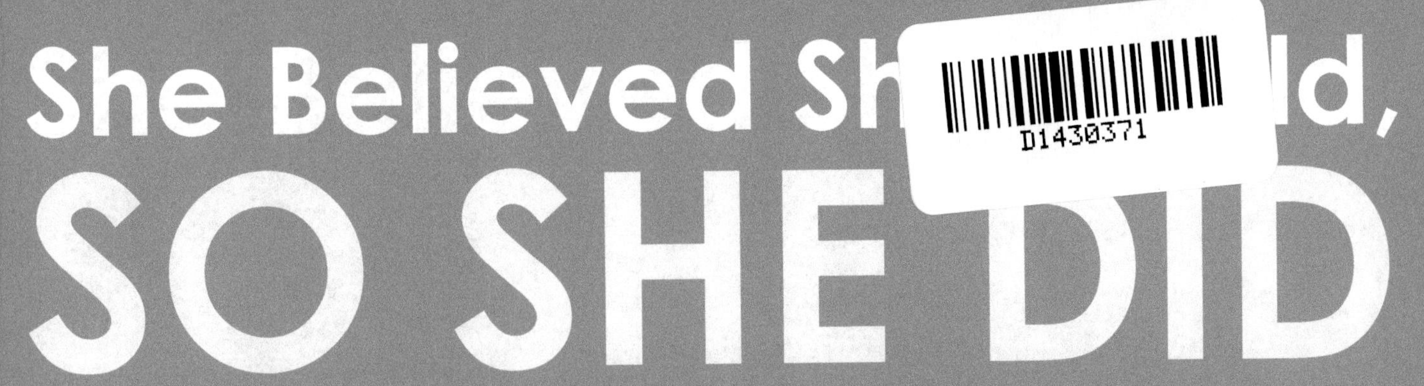

She Believed Sh ld,
SO SHE DID

Written by
Savannah Solis
Illustrated by Hunter Mooney

She Believed She Could, So She Did

ISBN:
978-1-63308-608-1 (hardback)
978-1-63308-609-8 (paperback)
978-1-63308-610-4 (ebook)

Illustrated by *Hunter Mooney*

CHALFANT ECKERT
PUBLISHING

1028 S Bishop Avenue, Dept. 178
Rolla, MO 65401

Printed in United States of America

She Believed She Could, SO SHE DID

Written by

Savannah Solis

Illustrated by Hunter Mooney

In memory of
Detective Liu and Detective Ramos
and all the men and women
who have paid the ultimate sacrifice
in the line of duty.

Dedicated to my hero,
Officer Victor Cabral
and Mrs. Madeline Cabral
for always praying for me and
encouraging me to keep shining.

Also for the best Mom and Dad ever.
Thank you for always telling me
to dream big.

There once was a girl
with a big, gigantic dream.

She dreamed
that one day
she would be
a police officer.

GROCERY

She loved police officers so much, because they helped people.

She dreamed that one day
she would protect people
just like her heroes.

POLICE K9

She couldn't wait to get
her very own police car
and hear all the loud sirens.

She wanted to serve people in her community just like her heroes.

STOP

She dreamed that one day
she would get to work
with her best friend.

BACK THE BLUE
We SUPPORT OUR POLICE
LOVE

She dreamed about wearing a shiny badge just like her heroes.

She dreamed that one day
she would make a lot of children smile,
even when they were scared,
because that's what police officers do.

She would help find lost children
and bring them back to their parents,
because that's what police officers do.

THANK YOU
THANK YOU!
THANK YOU!

She loved police officers
so much that she began making
thank you cards for them.

She had a dream
that she would meet
officers all over America.

She wanted to inspire others just like her heroes had inspired her.

She had a big dream,
and she found out that
if she was passionate enough
about following her dreams…

K9

ONE DAY
YOUR DREAMS
REALLY CAN
COME TRUE.

She Believed She Could,
So She Did.

Kissimmee Police Officer
Matthew Baxter, 27
E.O.W 8/18/17

Illustration by Officer Baxter's daughters, Sariah, Sarah and Sophia

Texas State Trooper
Damon Allen, 41
E.O.W 11/23/17

Illustration by State Trooper Allen's daughter
Madison

Florida State Trooper Chelsea Richard, 30 E.O.W 5/3/14

Illustration by State Trooper Richard's son, Clayton

POLICE DEPARTMENT
CITY OF NEW YORK
NYPD
THANK YOU
POLICE
NYPD

11.03.20

POLICE
THE
HEALING
SPRINGS
SHOW
Danke

HIGHWAY P
EANTS
ASSOCIATION
.P.D.
SERGEANTS BENEVOLE

THE STATE OF TEXAS
NYPD
We see
You

SAVANNAH & LEO
NYPD
45
Highlights
DIG IN!
Saying
"Thank You"
in a Big Way

Savannah Says

THANKS

#TheyMatterToMe

CPSIA information can be obtained
at www.ICGtesting.com
Printed in the USA
LVHW060037080720
660035LV00018B/2115